Toys ★ in Space

MINI GREY

RED FOX

That summer night
for the first time
the toys were left outside.

Toys in Space

Some other books by Mini Grey

Egg Drop
The Pea and the Princess
Biscuit Bear
The Adventures of the
Dish and the Spoon
Three by the Sea
Traction Man Is Here
Traction Man Meets Turbodog
Traction Man and the Beach Odyssey

For Janet Schulman

TOYS IN SPACE 978 1 849 41561 3
A RED FOX BOOK

First published in Great Britain by Jonathan Cape, an imprint of
Random House Children's Publishers UK
A Random House Group Company

Jonathan Cape edition published 2012
Red Fox edition published 2013

1 3 5 7 9 10 8 6 4 2

Copyright © Mini Grey, 2012

Red Fox Books are published by Random House Children's Publishers UK,
61–63 Uxbridge Road, London W5 5SA

www.randomhousechildrens.co.uk   www.randomhouse.co.uk

Addresses for companies within The Random House Group Limited
can be found at: www.randomhouse.co.uk/offices.htm

THE RANDOM HOUSE GROUP Limited Reg. No. 954009

A CIP catalogue record for this book is available from the British Library.

Printed in China

MIX
Paper from
responsible sources
FSC® C020056

The Random House Group Limited supports the Forest Stewardship Council® (FSC®), the leading international
forest certification organisation. Our books carrying the FSC label are printed on FSC®-certified paper. FSC
is the only forest certification scheme supported by the leading environmental organisations, including
Greenpeace. Our paper procurement policy can be found at www.randomhouse.co.uk/environment

The sun went down,

the sky grew dark,

and, for the very first time…

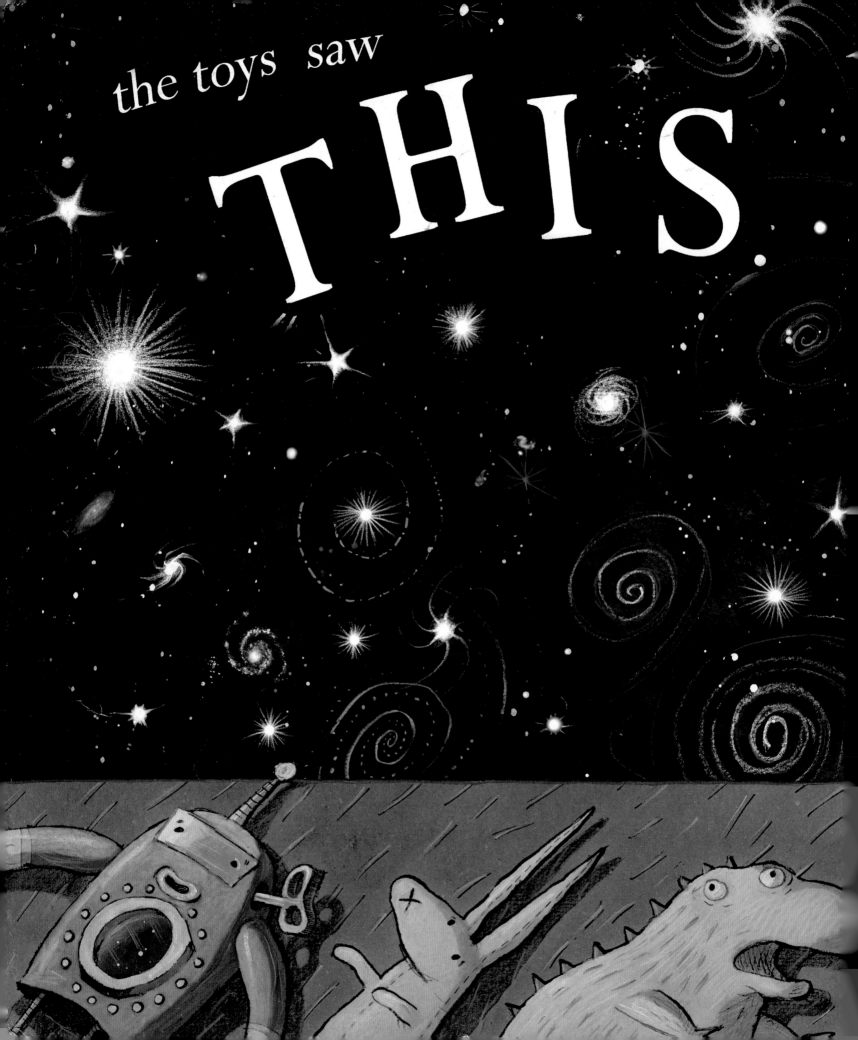

the toys saw

THIS

Everyone was quiet
for a while.

Once upon a time *(the WonderDoll said)* there were seven toys left out in the garden:

a resourceful Pink Horse,

a brave Small Sheep,

a clever Blue Rabbit,

a strong little Cowboy,

a thoughtful green Dinosaur,

a helpful wind-up Robot

and a WonderDoll.

Well, the sun went down and the toys saw the stars for the very first time.

And then one of the stars started to grow. It got bigger and bigger and bigger.

And the toys realised it
was actually not a star at all -
it was a space ship!

And the space ship
opened up a bright
hole and
beamed
the toys
up into it.

Well *(went on the WonderDoll)*, the toys were inside the spaceship and feeling a bit worried as you can imagine.

Then a door opened...

It's a drooling alien! It probably likes to eat pink felt!

It might drool at the toys!

No dang alien is drooling at me!

…and the toys saw a shadow in the doorway.

In came a space creature.

It looked carefully at all the toys.
None of the toys was the one it was looking for.

The Hoctopize showed the toys
a picture of its Cuddles who was
lost.

It took them to the Room of a Thousand Lost Toys.

It had collected them from gardens all over Earth.

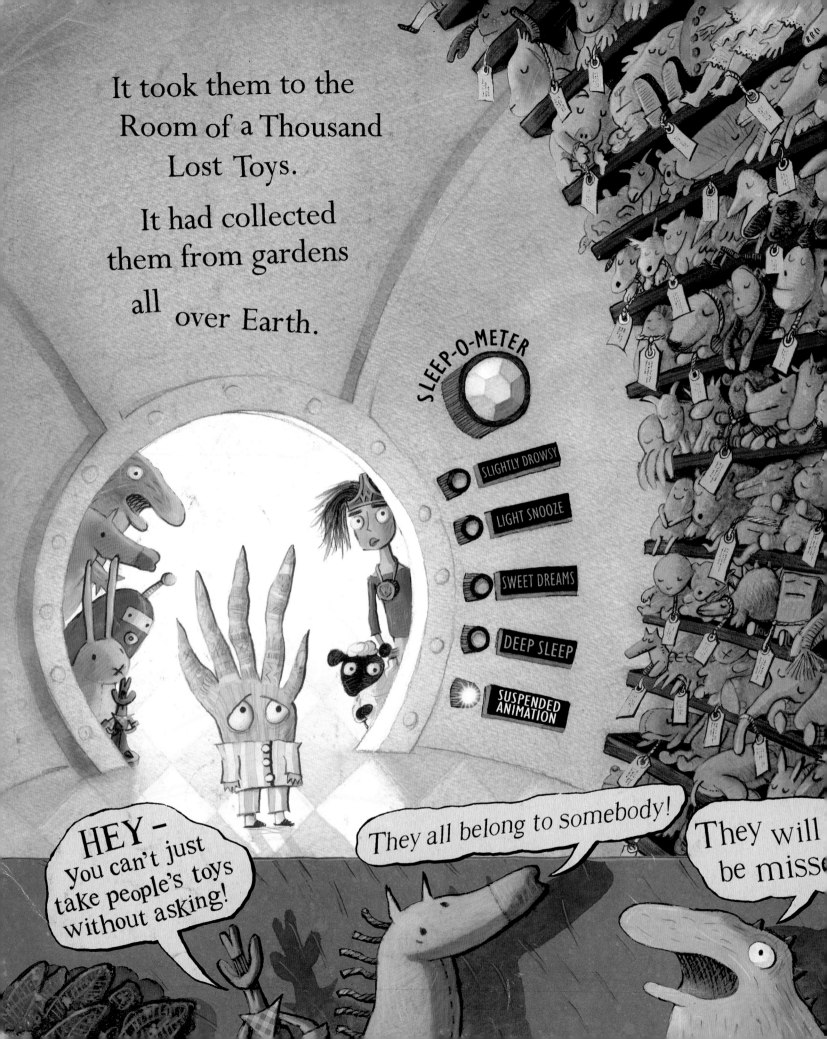

The toys helped the Hoctopize to realise that all those Thousand Lost Toys had to be returned to their real homes.

> But how do they know where to send them?

Luckily the Hoctopize was very organised and had labelled them all with their addresses.

It put a stamp on each label to help with the delivery.

Then they parachuted them all down towards Earth.

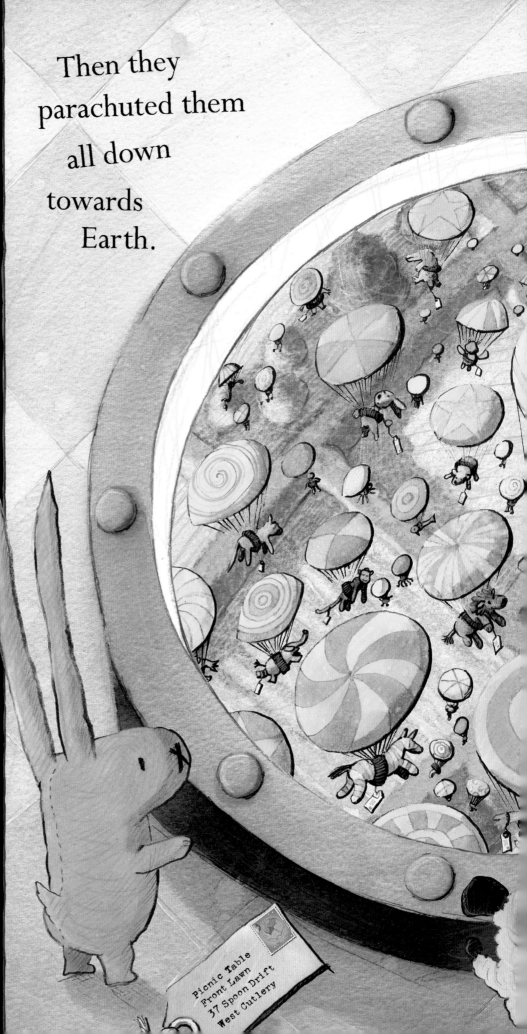

Once
they had gone,
the Hoctopize
sat down and cried.
It still didn't have
its Cuddles.

The toys need to
make it feel better!

Then the Dinosaur
had an idea – they
could have a party to
cheer up
the Hoctopize.

Everyone had jobs to do:
Blue Rabbit and Pink Horse made a cake,
WonderDoll and Small Sheep made party hats - and Robot and Dinosaur did the decorations.

And what about the Cowboy? What did the Cowboy do?

The Cowboy organised all the games.

Hey! You! **Stop!** You're out!

They played musical chairs and musical statues and pass-the-parcel.

It turned out
that the Hoctopize
was outstandingly good
at musical statues,

and won
every time.

What was the prize?

Our toys have to return
(the WonderDoll carried on).

They each hold a balloon to drift down,
and everybody takes a piece of cake.

The Hoctopize waves goodbye.

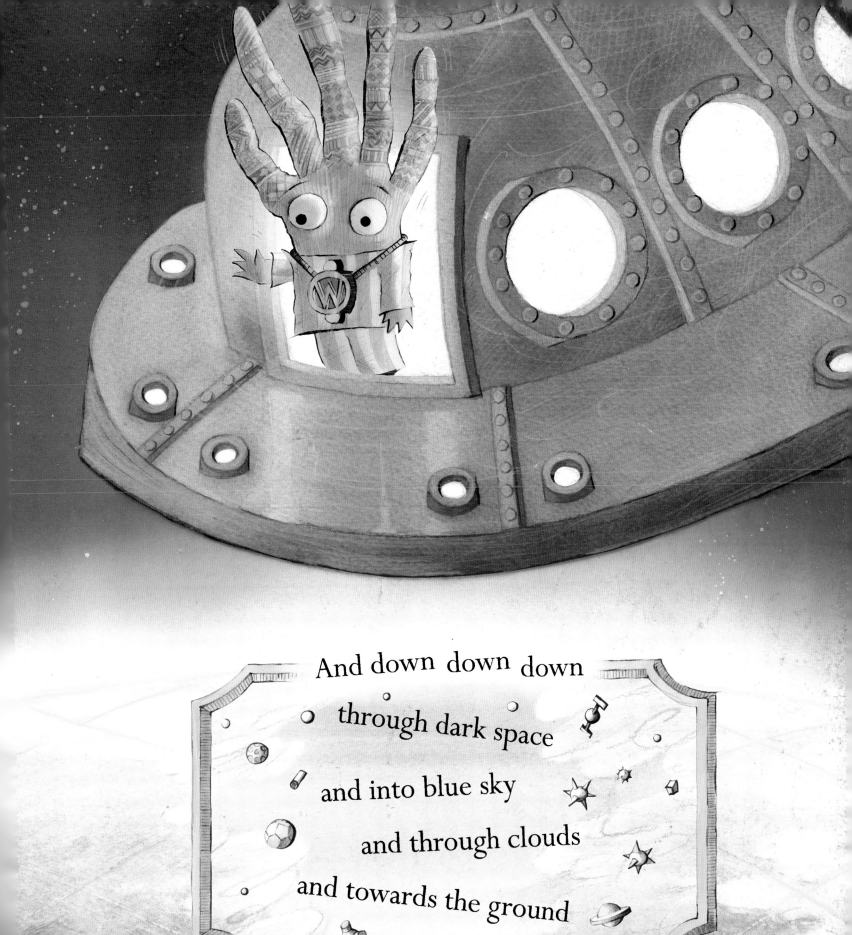

And down down down
through dark space
and into blue sky
and through clouds
and towards the ground
float the toys.

The WonderDoll stopped.

The toys opened
their eyes – the dawn
had happened.

It was a new day,
and soon they would
be found.

Oh yes (said the WonderDoll),
of course it will find its Cuddles.

BEAM-O-TRON

It will be
in the last
place it looks.

UP

DOWN

BEAMING

UP

DOWN

Things
always are.